THE LAST WAVE

John enjoyed sitting on the porch of a new home in Glenbrook. He and Elle had purchased their new, colonial-style home with money they had received from the sale of a townhouse in the nearby big city of Austin, Texas. The in-town home had certainly served its purpose – eliminating most of the nasty commuting most people who lived in suburbs had to endure. Glenbrook would have been affordable before they retired, but living in Glenbrook would have made each day's commute a nightmare.

While sipping a hot cup of coffee on this warm, early-summer morning, June 24, 2020, John could hear a symphony of birds calling for mates. He guessed they were males becoming desperate about not having found an available female during the spring mating season.

Children were out early riding their bikes around the cul-de-sac at the end of their street. The kids, as usual, were shrieking at one another. But, that noise did not disturb him. Noisy kids and singing birds confirmed his feeling that all was going well in Glenbrook.

Homes in Glenbrook were fashionable and cozy, but the cost of suburban real estate was not what one would call inexpensive. Land in this suburb of Austin had become very expensive. Builders spaced most of the homes on their cul-de-sac rather close to one another. On some mornings, like the one today, one could, if one tried, hear conversations from a nearby neighbor's porch.

This morning, their next door neighbor, Mrs. Terry Wright, was sitting on her porch. She was watering some of her potted plants while listening to a portable radio. John could barely hear the news reports coming from her radio. But, as usual, he had heard many of the news reports before and was able to fill in the words he was unsure were being reported. And, as usual the reports were depressing. As his friend Ray used to say, "Listeners do not want to hear about PTA meetings or church socials."

The news reports which John could overhear and make out today were often repeated every morning. One story told of the discovery of a new asteroid that astronomers were claiming they had recently found. The astronomers did not believe this asteroid would be a threat to Earth.

The following story dealt with recent protests that had begun to develop in some of America's big inner cities – including Austin. Unfortunately, peaceful protests had been contaminated by trouble makers, dope addicts, and criminals who had caused considerable damage to downtown properties by rock throwing and Molotov cocktails. Most suburbanites dismissed these events as stupid and ineffective.

The final story, before Mrs. Wright turned off her radio, reported vibrations having been detected by geologists in an area close to the Yellowstone Geyser. The scientists' reports had stated steam was leaking from an underground pocket of lava beneath Yellowstone Park. Expert geologists were discounting these events a "once-in-a-thousand-year" risk of an eminent eruption. John sipped his coffee and dismissed this news as "just more of the same."

John had always been a very sound sleeper. When he was in the Army, he had an extremely difficult time staying awake when it was his turn to stand guard. The on and off sleep pattern did not seem to be a problem for others, but he found himself nodding off – knowing that getting caught sleeping while on guard duty would most probably cost him a spell of confinement in the Army stockade.

Living in Glenbrook made sleeping soundly during the night an asset once again. Tonight, he had nodded off at around 9:00 PM. None the less, at about midnight, something had caused him to wake up. It was loud voices calling out demands for justice and due process. John had no idea what the voices were really all about, what it was the noise makers wanted, or why they had chosen his neighborhood for their protests. Why Glenbrook? As the cobwebs left his mind, he recalled the radio report he overheard from Mrs. Wright's porch. It could be the Austin trouble makers had moved to Glenbrook.

He reached for Elle, she was not in bed. But he heard her shuffling around in the living room adjacent to their bedroom. She was trying to call out to him in a horse-whisper.

"John, something bad is going on near the cul-du-sac; I think they are going to try burning us out. What shall we do?"

John kept his 45 cal pistol under their bed. He removed it – just in case. He horse-whispered in his answer to Elle.

"Turn out the lights. When it is light in here, they can see us, but we cannot see them."

Elle turned off all the living room lamps. They moved toward the smallest window in the living room and cracked open the blinds. They were now able to make out what appeared to be the same young thugs they had seen last week on the evening news – raising Hell in Austin. The demonstrators were carrying torches and placards.

John again whispered to Elle, even though it was doubtful the trouble makers would have been able to hear voices coming from inside their home.

"Sit tight and do not make noise, do not open the blinds any wider, and do not turn on any lights. The law allows us to defend ourselves. I will not allow anyone to enter our home."

Several trouble makers were moving closer to their house. He tried not to be anxious or nervous. Nerves of steel are needed for fleeing or fighting. He reminded himself that his 45 cal magnum pistol held six rounds. He knew how to use it. The thugs looked young, but they would be capable of using their placard poles as weapons and their torches to burn them out of their home. One should never under estimate an enemy. He was getting old. They were young and outnumbered him by at least five to one. He need to keep Elle silent and out-of-sight.

"Elle, please keep very quiet if they try to break in. Hide behind the chair in our bedroom. I'll handle this."

"Do you think they will try to kill us," she whispered.

"Not if I can help it. If I have to shoot one in the leg, the rest will run like rabbits."

The couple lay quietly on their living room floor. Elle got up, entered the bedroom and was behind a chair. He located himself in an area that gave him a clear view of their front door and sliding glass patio door. He knew both were locked. He made a point of checking each night before they turned in. Now, all they could do was wait. Maybe these nitwits would think no one was home – maybe they would assume the occupants were asleep. Maybe….

"John, someone just broke into the window in our study. Did you hear the glass breaking?"

"Yea, I heard it, but someone is trying to kick out our patio door. I wish you had a gun too."

"I don't think I could ever use it. Hopefully only one trouble maker will get in."

At that moment, the patio door shattered and someone stuck a leg through the broken glass. John had a good clear shot at that leg. That would do. The pain would stop any intruder, and the noise from his handgun would undoubtedly drive off the intruder trying to enter the broken patio door. He pulled the trigger. He heard the intruder scream out with pain and saw the leg moving while the intruder was trying to pulling it out of the glass. But, the leg only got half-way out of the broken glass. It appeared the intruder had passed out. The leg stopped moving. The intruder stopped screaming.

Elle shouted from the bedroom, "It's like you said John; as soon as your gun fired, the one trying to break into our study took off. Thank God."

John carefully approached the intruder who was now hanging by one leg from their patio door. He tried to see how badly the guy was hurt. He wanted to know what to tell the police when they arrived. He tried to find a pulse in the intruder's groin area. There is a large artery there; he believed the femoral artery ended there. He could not find a pulse.

"My God Elle. I think this guy is dead. His pants are soaked with blood, and I cannot find a pulse. I know our phone and modem cables have been damaged. I tried to call 911 there was no sound. Could you give me your cell phone?

Elle went back to their bedroom and returned with her cell phone. John called the police.

###

It took only a few minutes for two Glenbrook squad cars to arrive – lights flashing. John opened the front door and started to exit their home. He wanted to greet the officers, to explain.

"Stay where you are. We will come to you," shouted the heavy-set cop with his gun drawn. We want to look around for evidence and take some statements. Where is the dead guy?"

As the heavy policeman entered their home, he took the liberty of inviting his African-American partner in as well.

John, walked with the police officers through the living room to the patio door and pointed.

"Jesus, did you just let him hang there and bleed to death while you were waiting for us?"

John tried to explain, "Well, no. I took his pulse and knew he was already dead."

The thin black officer looked at John – not being able to hide his obvious anger. Then he asked, "Did you try CPR? You are not a doctor are you."

"Well no. Hey this guy was trying to enter our home in the middle of the night for Christ's sake"

"Sir, you're going to need to come down to the station to clear this up.?

"You must be kidding officer, you want me to come to the station and clear up the obvious fact that that this guy hanging in my window, in my home, at midnight, was wounded trying to break in our home, and his condition is my fault?"

The African-American cop looked over at the other cop who was talking to Elle, and called out to his partner, "Hey Frank, we have a wise ass here. He wants us to prove that he didn't let that poor dead brother bleed to death; because he, a rich white guy, was acting in self defense. What did his wife have to say?"

"She was in the other room. She is not going to be a witness. She can stay here. Let's get that poor devil out of their window and over to the medical examiner. Help me secure this dude with cuffs and put our suspect in a transport vehicle. We can meet them at the station."

John wanted to resist being arrested without a warrant and being handcuffed; but, he had been around long enough to know resistance would only make everything worse – for himself. The cops would like nothing better than to rough him up. And, a resisting arrest charge would almost insure a conviction – in spite of any proofs or his obvious innocence.

John found himself in a virtual cave. The rear doors of the squad car that was transporting him to the police station had its door handles removed. John's hands we cuffed behind his back. When he tried to make himself comfortable, the handcuffs dug into his wrists and seemed to get tighter. Between the rear seat area and the driver's seat a heavy wire mesh had been installed. Calling this a "transport vehicle" was police jargon for a "jail on wheels."

The police station was about a block away from the courthouse. The squad car pulled off the road and drove into a secure sally-port. A pair of steel overhead doors closed behind them. John now belonged to the police. Would this be how he would be living the rest of his days? He knew he had acted in self defense, but he had heard of innocent people spending many years incarcerated. He felt like a cork bobbing in water. He tried to remain composed but it was not easy.

The two police who escorted into the station were polite – but not sociable. They steadied him by his elbows to keep him from falling when he had stumbled on a stoop located near the closest entry door. Maybe these guys would be fair – maybe not. He wished he knew. Once inside, they walked down a narrow hall with doors on each side. The cops escorted him into a small room with a desk in the center. There were two folding chairs on one side of the desk – only one chair on the other side. There were no windows and only the one door.

There was a phone of some sort on the desk. This is where, he felt certain, the police would try to induce him to make a statement. At this point, they would be satisfied with any kind of conversation. If a suspect admits or denies a crime in a statement, as he well knew, it "could or would be used" against him. He noticed a camera in the corner near the ceiling. There appeared to be a two-way mirror on one wall.

The black cop, who had been the first to accuse him, now changed his tune. He tried to curry favors.

"Would you like a cup of coffee or a soda?"

"No, thank you."

"How about a smoke?

"No, thank you."

"Have a seat, over there. Frank O'Hara and I will sit on this side. I am Demetrius Jones, and yours?"

"John Ceres."

At this point, John expected an interrogation to begin. It did not. Both cops simply sat there looking at him. The room remained silent. John was not about to volunteer any statements. He would wait them out. He knew from the days when he practiced criminal law that the "silent treatment" is one of the most effective police interrogation techniques.

After about five minutes of silence that seemed an eternity, Officer Jones broke the silence.

"Don't you think it's about time you told us your side of what happened?"

"Gentlemen, you are wasting your time. I am not going to talk to you at this time."

"Hey, you can tell us what happened and go home or you can have us book you for manslaughter. It is up to you what happens."

"Am I free to leave?"

Officer Jones did not hesitate to answer, "Not until you tell us why we should."

"Okay, I'll consider myself to be under arrest. I want a lawyer."

###

John did not even remember being booked or escorted to his cell. But, his mind began to clear when he began to look around his steel cage. Nearly everything was made of metal – the sink, toilet bowl, bed, table, and seats anchored to the concrete floor. He learned from a prisoner in an adjacent cell that, just before lights out, the guards would bring a mattress and blanket to put on his bed. They would collect them in the morning.

John was told by fellow prisoners there would be no pillow. Most guys used their bundled up shirt for a pillow. There would be a time each day when a guard would bring a bar of soap, towel, and toothbrush for each prisoner. After cleaning up, the guards would collect what was left of this hygiene material. There would be a shower provided two times each week.

John sat on one of the steel seats the jail provided, he placed his forearms on his knees, and looked at the concrete floor. It was beginning to sink in, that unless his bail was set in a reasonable amount, this would be his new way of life. He felt a tsunami size wave of depression sweep over him. He would use his one phone call to Elle in the morning. She could be able help him employ a criminal defense lawyer. Only a fool defends himself – even if he himself had once practiced criminal law. She would also be able to post a reasonable bail bond. There house was paid for. It would probably be adequate collateral. And, he needed to advise Elle to avoid verbosity during his calls from jail. Calls are recorded.

"Hear Yo, Hear Yo, the 356th District Court of Lee County, Texas is now in session. Maintain silence, please. Cell phones will be confiscated if they interrupt these proceedings," called out the elderly, over weight bailiff, as the African-American judge entered the courtroom from his chambers.

"Take your seats, please. This is the case of State of Texas v. John Ceres set for the defendant's first appearance and bail setting for the charged offense of Manslaughter. Is the State ready?"

"Yes Your Honor. The defendant has not been indicted. The Grand Jury meets next week. The sworn complaint by Officer Jones, alleges the defendant allowed the victim to bleed to death after shooting him with his 45 cal pistol. The State is asking that his bail be set at $500,000. This matter will be set for status of attorney next Friday. By then, we should have a True or No Bill from the Grand Jury."

COURT: "The defendant is hereby granted three phone calls. Bail at this time is set at $500,000 – cash or surety. Court is adjourned."

Back in his steel cage, John managed to drift off into a troubled sleep in spite of his lumpy-shirt, improvised pillow and grimy mattress. He was not allowed to have his wrist watch in his cell. Nevertheless, at sometime close to 10:00 PM, with his body clock usually being fairly accurate, John was awakened by many loud voices. The voices did not sound as if they were coming from inside the jail. He reasoned something was going on outside.

John called out to the guard on duty, "Hey jailer, if you can hear me? What is going on?"

An overweight, scruffy, probably a retired cop, came down the hall to John's cell area, "Don't worry. Those trouble makers from Austin will not be able to get in here to cause us any harm. They are mostly young, black high-school drop outs – like the ones that broke into your house. They are, for the most part, poorly armed. This jail was built to survive an Apache Indian attack."

"Thank you for the information. What are they so hot about?"

"You killed one of them. They have been blaming all white folks for our few police extremists and their maltreatment of their young, black lawbreaker friends; and those poor innocent kids whose parents never told them not to resist even an illegal arrest, or lip off to a cop who stops them for questioning. It will not be good for you – now that you are on their shit list. You better be careful. Lay low."

"Surely you're kidding. The guy I shot was trying to get into our house – with a torch – after breaking our patio door window. I'm the damned victim."

"Don't tell me. I am just here to make sure they do not break in and get their hands on you. Only God knows what they would do. They are a bunch on know-it-all nitwits. They harass us more than we harass them. Try to get some rest. You'll be safe – at least tonight."

"Hey, thanks again. Thanks for filling me in."

John returned to his cot and tried to sleep. He did not rest until the outside shouting stopped at about 2:00 AM. What he learned was valuable. The only encouraging words John had heard were to be found in the guard's describing the incident at his home... the guard had heard John and Elle had been victims of a break in by young thugs from Austin. Maybe potential jurors had heard the same version.

###

John woke up before reveille. He was hungry and could no longer sleep. He sat up on his cot and waited. When the guards called out reveille, they took a head count. John knew that was standard procedure. There is seldom an escape from confinement. When the police corporal reached John's cell, he stopped and said with a grin, "You will not be dining with us this morning. Your wife has posted your bail. I don't know what she sees in you. Ha. Ha."

"So, am I free to leave?"

"I wouldn't be so anxious to leave here, if I were you. Did you hear that mob of misfits from Austin raising Hell last night? Well, when they find out this afternoon that you are out of here, guess where they will go to look for you? You and your wife need to board up your house and go somewhere else. Of course, you must keep your bail bondsman informed of your whereabouts. I don't envy you bud."

"Thanks for the advice. When will I be released?"

"Well, it is 6:30 now. The Sheriff's office staff does not get here until 7:00. You should hit the street at around 8:00. You can call your wife in a few minutes. But, tell her not to broadcast your release. Those nitwits from Austin usually sleep in until about noon. But they all have cell phones and people who could tip them off regarding your early release. They would probably come looking for you."

"Couldn't the Sheriff provide me with some protection?"

"Nah, we sometimes do that for some high-profile State's witnesses. You would have to hire your own protection. We are holding your weapons as evidence. Besides, you would prove to everyone that you are nuts if you were to shoot someone else. Hey, get a can of wasp spray. It can hit a target at 15-20 feet away. And, the dude on the receiving end would be disabled for about an hour."

"I cannot thank you enough for your help. What is your name?"

"Corporal Johnson, Badge 231. Now, let's go call your wife."

###

John called Elle and, after thanking her for making bail for him, told her not to tell anyone else about the details of his release. He also told her he would fill her in on a few other things she needed to know – reminding her that all jail phone calls and visitor conversations are tape recorded.

"Okay Honey, but you are beginning to sound like a criminal."

"Please Elle, let's wait and talk about this when I get home. When will you be ready to pick me up? The Sheriff's Corporal Johnson says I can be released by 8:00."

"Okay. Goodbye Honey. I will see you at 8:00."

###

Corporal Johnson was in the Sheriff's business office when John finally got released at about a quarter to eight. He spotted John and walked over to see him.

"You have a good woman. She got here about 7:30 and has been waiting in the lobby. Remember what I told you. You want to make sure she is safe – and that applies to you as well. Maybe she can stay with her family for awhile. Then, it would be easier for you to hide out from the Austin 'gang banger' crowd."

John picked up the plastic bag that contained all the items the police removed from him during his initial confinement. He opened it and found his wallet, wrist watch, keys, coins, and cell phone. He opened the wallet and checked his credit cards, business cards, and the $55.00 he had usually kept in his wallet. "Everything is cool," he thought to himself.

"When can I leave?

"As soon as you sign this receipt. Here is the stuff from the probation department – that will be your new Bible. Read those rules carefully. If you screw up, the probation department will advise the judge. He will issue an arrest warrant."

John signed the receipts, one for his personal items and one for the new rules from the probation department. He headed for the lobby where he knew Elle was waiting. When he opened the lobby door, he saw Elle waiting patiently. She looked tired. She did not have any makeup on. But, he thought she still looked beautiful. He felt guilty for having caused her so much trouble.

"Hi Sweetie, you cannot imagine how happy I am to see you."

"John, I really missed you. I did not go back to our house. I stayed with my sister Phyllis last night. It helped a little. The car is parked around the corner. The lot is only for county people. It was very disturbing having to pledge our home for your bail. You must feel the same way."

"For sure, we worked hard to find it and make it our nest. Let's get in the car and talk. These jail walls may have ears."

John opened the passenger door for Elle. She told him many times that he need not do so, but he knew she liked it. Once he got into the car, John looked Elle in the eyes and prepared to give her the bad news he had received from the jailers.

"Honey, we have been warned by the Sheriff's deputies to find another place to stay while we wait for the trial. They think the Austin gang banger crowd will try to find us and seek revenge. I thought we could look into a motel or an extended stay place. But, they would be extremely costly when used for a longish time - when added to what we will have to pay my attorney. What about your sister Phyllis? We could pay her and Bruce, chip in on the food and extra utilities – maybe pay a little rent."

"Oh John, I would not want to do that. It would not be fair for them to suffer too."

"What if you stay with them; I can crash almost anywhere. I got used to Army housing, I can deal with it."

"But, that would mean we would have to be apart – for the first time since we got married."

"How about selling the house, using some of the cash for a cash bond, for my attorney, and using the rest for another place? Would that work?"

"I think so, but what a bummer. We worked so hard and now nearly all our efforts seem to be going up in smoke. For now, let's go to Phyllis and Bruce's place. But, remember, on the bond you signed, you promised to keep the probation department advised on your whereabouts. Us being apart would not help. Your location is going to be a public record. If the hoods from Austin find us there, I am sure Phyllis's husband has several guns for self-defense."

"Yea, then he could join me and be locked up and financially ruined for self defense," he cynically quipped.

###

Phyllis and Bruce were cordial when they greeted John and Elle. Nevertheless, having practiced law for many years before retirement, John had developed an ability to read facial expressions, eye contact, and body language. It seemed to him Elle's sister and especially her brother-in-law were not exactly happy about their new tenants.

John tried to mitigate their displeasure, "We do not intend to impose on your hospitality for very long. We know how you must feel. But, rest assured, we do not intend to hide out here and cost you any financial burden. We want to help out with your expenses and we will respect your privacy."

Phyllis quickly smiled and tried to assure them, "Hey, Elle is my sister. We are happy to help you both through this crisis. I feel certain you would do the same for us. Let me show you our guest room. I think you will like it. It has a full private bath."

John and Elle followed Phyllis down a rather long hallway. The guest bedroom was located at the end of the hall. It was a little small – as was its adjacent, full bath. It was certainly a whole lot better than the typical smallish motel rooms they had occasionally rented – once in awhile – for only one night. But, that is what one would expect in this downsized home which Bruce and Phyllis had purchased to replace their prior, much larger place – after the kids turned them into empty nest retirees. John, thought to himself, they might not be staying here very long. At least, that is what he was silently thinking.

Elle gave her sister a big hug. Phyllis smiled and kissed Elle on the cheek. "You know I love you Sis."

John could see that hug and those kind words meant a lot to Elle. She smiled and John could see tears welling up in her eyes. He felt guilty for having put them all in such a bad spot. He wished he had never pulled that trigger. He needed to sell their house as soon as possible. They would never again be safe there. Maybe they could find a small house or apartment in Austin. He knew he could set up a trust to keep their location secret from the Austin street gangs who would now be looking for revenge.

It was a typical, clear, hot, Austin, Texas day when John and Elle went looking for an apartment. Bruce and Phyllis had both reassured them that they were welcome to stay as long as they wished. But, looking for an apartment became more urgent once John reminded Bruce, Phyllis, and Elle that it would not be safe for them to do so.

Bruce had turned white as a ghost when John, out of respect for everyone's safety, advised them, that it was his opinion, Bruce and John could not chance a shootout with a mob of Austin hoods. If the hoods won, John, Bruce, and maybe their wives might end up dead. If John and Bruce won, it could end up with both finding themselves in jail.

Even in Texas, the days when self-defense was once deemed a God given right, was disappearing. The bleeding hearts in the USA were convincing more and more people that even violent protesting was Constitutionally protected and trumped the right to use weapons in self defense.

Everyone had agreed to let John use Bruce's and Phyllis's home address on his bail paperwork and keep the new apartment secret. Elle recommended that they not use a real estate salesperson. Any bad actors looking for them would check out commercial apartment complexes and real estate agents first.

At around 10:00 AM, Elle was seated in the bucket seat next to John with the Real Estate section of *The Austin Gazette*. She was reading the apartments for rent items to him as he drove. It was already 80 degrees. By this afternoon, the temperature would probably exceed 100. Elle read the apartment ads out loud.

Near Lake Austin, 2 BR, 2 BA, on 2nd or 3rd floor, close to near Jefferson Davis School, close to shopping and Capital, $2,000 - $2,500 per month with 12 month lease. Call 512-777-4250. Great View, on shore of Lake Austin, 1 BR, 1 BA, Quiet, Clean, 1st Floor with 12-13 month lease. $1,200 - $1,300 per month. Call 512-777-4250.

John interrupted, "Since we are using this as a temporary hideout, I would think the one bedroom place would do. What do you think?"

"I guess it would be Okay. Let's give this guy a call. Looks like he owns both – or is agent for both."

###

At around noon, they pulled into a small parking lot where they had been directed to come to by a bubbly female who had answered the phone listed in the ads. The small office building wasn't covered with real estate signs. It was obviously not a big time real estate office. The girl who greeted them had the same voice as the gal who had answered the phone.

"We are here to see Mr. Jackson. You may remember you helped us set up an appointment with him," Elle said after she identified herself and John.

"Of course, have a seat; Mr. Jackson called, he will be here in four of five minutes."

Elle and John sat in a couple of well-used chairs near the front window facing the parking lot. About three – four minutes later, a black, late-model, Cadillac Escalade pulled in and parked. A middle-aged black man with a cigar in his mouth got out and headed toward the office.

"You must be Mr. Jackson," John said, breaking the silence.

"So, you two must be the couple looking for an apartment? Let's go in my office. Would you like some coffee or soda?"

Elle answered, "Thanks for the offer, but we already had a couple of Pepsi Colas on the way. We were thinking about renting that one bedroom apartment you had listed in the *Gazette*."

"Whoa, I am glad you came to me for help. But John, me boy, I recognize you from the pictures in the newspapers and TV. Aren't you the guy that's charged with shooting one of the misfits from Austin who tried to break in your house?"

"Yea, you have a good eye for faces. So you can't help us?"

"Now son, I didn't say I can't help you. I just don't want to rent you either of those two apartments you saw in the paper – not for a year. I am looking for stable, employed tenants – not lawsuits and sad outcomes – not to mention those gangs read the papers, too. They could easily track you two down to do you harm. But, I can rent you what might work as a hideout – on a month-to-month basis. Of course, it would be in a part of town you might not like as much. It would be $2,500/month cash on the barrel head – no questions asked. Do you want to take a look see?"

Elle answered for John, "We really don't have a lot of options. When can we see the place?"

"Well, we are all standing here doing nothing. How about I drive you two over there now?"

Jackson grabbed his Dallas Cowboy baseball hat and picked up his car keys. He waddled toward the exit. As he passed his secretary's desk, he told her, "Sweetie, I'll be back in about 45 minutes or so."

John got into the passenger side of the Escalade – next to Mr. Jackson. He could smell the residue from Jackson's cigars even though no one was smoking. Elle got in the back seat.

As they drove away from the Austin Lake area, John thought Jackson was driving way too fast. But, he said nothing. He simply tightened his seat belt. Mr. Jackson noticed, "Scared? Don't worry. I'm a damned good driver. We don't have very far to go."

John looked in the back seat. Elle was tightening her seat belt too. They each knew what the other was thinking. About two miles down the road leaving the lake area, Jackson turned onto a narrow road that was sporting a few pot holes that one usually sees up North – usually caused by freezing ice. Another half mile brought them to a small house that looked a little run down. Some of the paint was pealing off the wood siding and the grass, using the term loosely had some weeds showing since it had not been mowed for awhile.

"Well folks, it ain't Glenbrook, but I think this is what you will be needing."

Elle answered first, "Let's take a look inside. Maybe it will work."

Jackson used his keys to unlock the front door. John and Elle followed Jackson into the house. They entered the living room. It was furnished with some furniture that looked well-used. But, Elle thought to herself, it could look better with a good cleaning. They all walked down a short hallway. Jackson opened the door to a rather small bedroom that had one dresser and a double bed. Elle didn't even want to imagine what hankie pankie had taken place on that bed. But, she could make sure it was bug free – before they used it. And, she would be able to brighten it up with bed coverings they already had.

Across from the bedroom there was another door. This one opened into a small bathroom. The toilet, sink, and tub all needed some strong cleaning agents. The tile floor was in pretty good shape. It was "functional."

The kitchen was simply a galley type of limited value. The stove needed cleaning, the refrigerator was small but fairly new. The sink was just that a galley sink. There was an exit door at the end of the kitchen area. They could survive if they carried out and ate on the small folding table with folding chairs in the corner of the kitchen.

Elle noticed John was checking all the windows and doors for security. She asked, "Does it look safe? Shouldn't we change the locks?"

John looked at Jackson and asked, "Could you put a deadbolt locks on the living room and kitchen doors? I can place pieces of wood into the window tracks to make them safer."

"Yea, we can do that; but, it's $2,500/month, month-to-month, COD. So, let's go back to the office."

When the Escalade pulled into the parking lot in front of Jackson's office, the parking lot was empty except for an older model Saturn that probably belonged to his secretary whom Jackson had previously called "Sweetie." She appeared to be in her mid-thirties. She was not wearing an engagement or wedding ring. Elle speculated, to herself, that "Sweetie" was probably a divorcee. But, since she was driving an old Saturn, she had probably not slept her way into her job. Elle speculated Jackson's secretary might someday prove to be a source of gossip that might prove useful to John and her in the future.

Once inside the office, Mr. Jackson spoke first. "Pam, I believe these two will be renting the property on 708 Travis Street for $2,500 per month – COD – without a lease. Isn't that right folks?" Jackson said, with a smile, while he looked at John.

John glanced at Elle who nodded "yes," but with a troubled look that John knew really meant, "I guess so."

Jackson spoke again, "They'll be giving you $2,500 cash – a money order or a cashier's check will do. It is okay to give them a cash receipt. You should expect them to come in the first of each month with another payment. And, have Julio put dead bolt locks on both doors later this afternoon."

Elle opened her purse and pulled out a partially completed $2,000 money order. She handed it to Pam who immediately noticed the money order was $500 short. So, Elle went on to explain, "We thought we could find something suitable for $2,000. But, we can provide the rest in cash."

Elle pulled out her wallet, opened it, and peeled five hundred dollar bills off of a rather large roll. As she handed the money to Pam, she simply said, "Here. Please give me a receipt and a set of keys."

"Julio will bring the keys to our office as soon as he finishes installing the new locks. You can stop by and pick them up about 4:30; he should be done by then," Jackson added.

John felt very proud of the way Elle had handled this entire housing matter. She was always thinking ahead – thinking of everything. He realized that, without her help, his problems could have been a hell of a lot worse. It was about 1:30 when they left Jackson's office. They would come back for the keys at 4:30. John suggested they stop somewhere nearby to have some coffee or soda – while they made some detailed plans.

"Well sweetheart, Jackson proved himself. He told me he had Julio install dead bolt locks on both doors. I was surprised he did. And, he gave us the keys yesterday, as he promised he would. I slept pretty well last night – in spite of that small double bed with the lumpy mattress. Those solid wooden doors, with those new locks, helped me feel safe for the first time in what now seems like an eternity.

"And I found it pretty easy to secure those windows. I had the guys at the hardware store cut strong wooden poles to fit all four windows. We are lucky the windows slide in tracks. No one can sneak in by sliding our windows open. They would have to break in – giving us time to prepare and protect ourselves – if we happened to be home. Of course, whenever we leave it could be a different story. Hell, crooks can break into banks. Nothing is 100% safe."

Elle looked concerned, "John, I hope your shooting people days are over – even in self defense."

"Not to worry. The probation officers made me deliver my guns to the sheriff's office – as a condition of my bail bond. But, while I was at the hardware store, I did buy a machete. I'm way too old to fight young thugs who are wearing tennis shoes bare handed. We are both too young to die."

"Hey, pay attention to the road. That building on the left is the probation office," she answered.

John tapped the brakes and turned into the probation parking lot. They got out rather quickly and locked their car. Unlike other county buildings, the probation office was not at all fancy. It was a cinder-block building with a sign on the door. Together, John and Elle read the notice taped to the door.

Before you enter this office, please wear a mask and stand at least six feet from any non-family member. Your temperature will be taken by the security officer and he or she will make sure you have no symptoms of corona virus. Once that screening is complete, please sign in with your name. If you have a family member, attorney, or bail bondsman with you, they must also sign in.

John's probation officer was a young, black female. She was far more friendly than they had anticipated. Her main concerns were weapons, possible drug use, and any new arrests. John filled out a form wherein he stated, under penalty of perjury, that all of his weapons were in the sheriff's custody, that he used no drugs, and had no new arrests.

"Of course, you know we will ask you to provide a urine sample. Here is your specimen bottle – with your name and case number on it. Please step into the washroom and provide a urine sample – in the presence of a male probation officer who would be able to testify it is your sample. Any problem with any of that?"

"None."

"Okay. Then, after you finish, seal the bottle and deliver it to the witness who attends the procedure."

"Okay."

John completed the process, answered a few questions, and turned in his forms.

John's probation officer approved his release and supporting paperwork. "You are free to leave. But, make sure you let us know if you move from your Glenbrook home. You must keep us informed of your whereabouts."

"Well, in fact we have moved to a less-expensive home. I'll write it down for you. But, please do not give it to anyone without a need to know – that would be your office and the sheriff's office. We have been threatened by friends and family of that jerk who tried to break into our Glenbrook home. It is one of the reasons we decided to move. We now use a P. O. Box for our mail. We no longer live in the Glenbrook home."

"Mr. Ceres, I'm pleased to have this new information. However, in the future, let us know BEFORE you move anywhere. Good luck to you and Mrs. Ceres."

###

On the way to what was to be their new home, John asked Elle if she felt they had been treated well by the Probation Department.

"I think it went about as well as could be expected. How often do you think you will have to report? They were nice enough but didn't you feel disrespected? I sure did."

Elle was looking at John while they were driving. John always kept his eyes on the road. But, before he could answer, Elle whispered.

"John, it may be my imagination, but I could swear there is a car full of young, black kids following us. Take a look in your rear-view mirror – without being obvious you are looking at them."

John glanced in his rear-view mirror. He saw a black, low rider Chevy Camaro following about three car lengths behind. It looked like there were at least four young thugs in their car. He suspected they may have seen him leaving the probation office. Logically, he thought, that would be the best place to find him. They would know, from their own contacts with the law, that an accused who is released on bond would be required to report. They probably had the place staked out. He knew they weren't going to such trouble for any lawful reason. They probably were seeking revenge for that home invader John fatally shot in the leg. However, he did not want to frighten Elle.

"John, I think you are going the wrong way. I believe this road leads back to the Courthouse Complex. Why did you turn back there?"

He realized it would not be fair to keep Elle in the dark about such a serious matter. He filled her in on his suspicions. He explained the safest place to go right now would be the Sheriff's Office. There would be deputies on duty who might be able to help.

As he pulled into the Courthouse parking lot, he could see the Camaro peal off in the opposite direction. Yet, he decided to tell Elle it would be best if they reported the stalking – to file a police report.

When they entered the Sheriff's business office, a Hispanic deputy greeted them. The deputy was typing as John dictated an incident report. When she finished, she handed them a copy.

"My name is Cindy Cortez. My badge number is on your copy. Call us if you have more trouble."

Elle chimed in, "Is there any way you could provide police protection?"

"No Ma'am. We have all the problems we can handle already. Austin is not the city it used to be. At night, we have large bands of thugs and trouble-makers downtown near the Capital building. From 11PM until dawn, it is like a war zone down there. I gave up rank to get this desk job. I have two small niños at home. I do not want them growing up without their mother."

Elle was quick to point out, "But, that leaves us alone in our new home – that we rented in order to hide out from these troublemakers."

"Don't let them follow you there. If they follow you, drive to any police station. Show them a copy of that report just I gave you. That will help. If they find your new home, you have the right to use self-defense measures."

"Well, that is how we got in this mess."

John added, "Maybe the squad car patrolling that area could swing by from time to time. Oh, by the way, thanks for all your help."

"No problema. That is what they pay us for. Call me if you have any questions. I will help – if I can."

John examined the area in and around the police parking lot. The Camaro that had been tailing them was now nowhere in sight.

"Honey, I think we should take a different way to our new hideout. It figures that those thugs in the Camaro would not be in this area – so close to the police station. But, they might be thinking we would take the same route back. So, let's take that other access road. It is in pretty bad condition, but it should be the safest way home – given the current situation. What do you think?"

"Sounds like a good plan. Please drive slowly. We would not want to get a flat tire on one of those pot holes."

"Will do."

Their car bounced around quite a bit on the way home; but, they got to their new house without any blow outs or flattened tires. They parked their car behind the house – there it would not be easy to be seen from the road. In the unlikely event the thugs in the Camaro somehow managed to find them, he was confident he would be able to deal with them from inside their home. Nevertheless, he was pretty sure he and Elle would not be found here.

John was satisfied with their two exterior doors and their new deadbolt locks. Before t He fortified their small windows, it would have been easy to gain entry – now he had inserted oak rods into the channels on which the windows slid to be opened. If anyone managed to break the glass to enter, he had his new machete and the benefit of knowing the layout of their home in the darkness of night.

###

"John, I am surprised we had such a peaceful night. It was nearly as quiet out here as it was in our Glenbrook home. I'm proud of the way we outfoxed those thugs that were trying to follow us. But, I am sorry to say I think we may have to live as fugitives until your case is resolved."

"I know. And, what about the fact that I need to physically report to probation once each month? And, what about our going out for groceries or buying gas for our car?"

A frown appeared on her face; John could always tell when she was thinking. They had been married a long time. He admired her quick, logical mind and her knack for finding solutions to problems.

"John, what if we do our shopping and report to probation in the early morning? These bums are usually creatures of the night. They are likely to come out after dark – when witnesses cannot see them. They are usually still tired when the sun comes up, they sleep during the late mornings and early afternoons."

"Good plan, but it is not 100%. Let's try it. But, it wouldn't hurt to wear different clothes than we commonly do. I'll go as a pirate and you as a dance hall gal," he answered with a smile.

For the first time in what seemed to be a long while, Elle cracked a broad smile. "You never lose your sense of humor do you? But, I agree, changing our appearance just might help."

###

John left the house by the back door in order to bring the car around for Elle. He was wearing a baseball cap that he had not used in several years. He was wearing Levi jeans and a sleeveless T-shirt which revealed a tattoo he had received while in the military. It was on his upper arm. He did not look like the retired lawyer from Glenbrook.

Elle dug out a mini-skirt she had worn to a recent Glenbrook neighborhood costume party. She had to fish it out of a cardboard moving box. She was wearing a University of Texas T-shirt. She didn't look like a suburban wife. He noticed how really young she looked for her age. Her legs were shapely, she had a youngish face, and even without a bra, one could see shapely mounds where her breasts were located.

"Who is the hot babe in a mini-skirt?"

She laughed. She knew time had been kind to her. "I'm with that young buck with the tattoo and baseball cap."

They had no problem during their junket to the HEB grocery store. It was a super store with gas pumps. They needed to fill their gas tank. HEB would be the easiest place to do it. Once the tank was full, John went to the cashier and paid with cash. His name was on his credit cards. He had learned how to be "on the lamb" from his clients who had jumped bail. Of course, he also remembered all of them were eventually caught.

As they drove home, Elle came up with another idea, "Why don't we leave this car at my sister's house and rent one that looks a lot different? At this point, saving money is not our goal."

"Sounds good to me. We can rent one from that 'Rent a Junk' place. By the month, it really would not cost too much."

At the Rent a Junk lot, they found a seven year old Chevy Impala that looked well-used. A salesman could not hide his displeasure with their choice. He asked himself, "How can I make a living renting out such cars?"

John resisted the sales pitch, "I know you must be wondering why we are renting this junk; but, we have to sell our Toyota Camry. I lost my job due to the corona virus lock down. We can't afford to keep it – even though we love it."

"I hear you. Why do you think I am working here? It's not what you would call a great place to work. But, I have kids and wife to feed. I can lease it to you for $8.00 per day on a month to month basis."

"Sounds fair to me," Elle chimed in.

Elle's sister, Phyllis, and her husband, Bruce, looked shocked when Elle explained their plans to her sister. But, they agreed to store the Toyota in one of their two garages. It had a few things in it, but it was fairly easy for John and Bruce to make room for the extra car.

After leaving Phyllis' house in their Chevy Impala the fugitive couple were in agreement. They had greatly decreased the chance of being found by the thugs from Austin.

The couple were certainly not happy with their new life. But, the Chevy seemed to be working well enough; and, after a few nights, they began to feel safe in their rented house.

Their family lawyers, Bolton and Wakely, had transferred ownership of their Glenbrook home to a blind trust. Mr. Benjamin Bolton, a friend of John's, agreed to act as the executor –

without a fee. They would only need to pay filing fees and secretarial time. Now, they started the arduous process of waiting for John's trial.

Mr. William "Bill" Wakely was the trial lawyer in the Bolton and Wakely law firm. Mr. Bolton was on the glide path to early retirement and had stopped doing trial work. Wakely had been a criminal and divorce lawyer and was known to be competent in both fields. He agreed to take John's case for a $10,000.00 retainer. John considered that expensive, but fair. He had to remind Elle that before he had retired he too had charged similar pricey retainers. Yet, he agreed with Elle when she said, "We are spending money as fast and easy as our Congress."

###

The Lee County Courthouse was not located in Austin, Texas. Had it been, John's case would have been filed in Travis County. Travis County was populated with many "Yankees" who had moved to Texas to escape the high taxes found in Northern states, Eastern states, and the poorly-managed State of California – which had the worst tax laws in the nation. Most of these folks considered themselves "liberal minded" and superior to native Texans like John.

The other big groups of potential jurors were "people of color" that included African Americans and first and second generation Mexican immigrants. Trying cases in Travis County often ended in plea agreements or hung juries. Jurors too often found a way to line up along racial, political, and economic lines. Texas not too long ago had been a Democrat stronghold. With the new immigrants, it had changed to Republican. Needless to say, trying cases in Travis County was often referred to as a "crap shoot."

John's lawyer, Bill Wakely, said he was happy the case had ended up in Lee County. He felt strongly that guilt or innocence often depended on the composition of the jury. John had also tried cases and could not agree more. In the suburban Lee County, where Glenbrook was located, most of the residents were educated commuters or retired folks like John and Elle. Most of them believed in guns and self-defense. If John wanted to win his trial, Lee County was a better venue than Travis. But, Bill and John both knew there is always the danger of "sleeper" being chosen for jury service – anywhere. And, the U. S. Supreme Court made sure it would prove very difficult to screen jurors based on race, sex, or national origins.

(*Batson v. Kentucky*, 476 U. S. 79, was a landmark decision of the US Supreme Court ruling that a prosecutor's use of a peremptory challenge in a criminal case—the dismissal of jurors without stating a valid cause for doing so—may not be used to exclude jurors based solely on their race. The Court ruled that this practice violated the Equal Protection Clause of the Fourteenth Amendment. The case gave rise to the term Batson challenge, an objection to a peremptory challenge based on the standard established by the Supreme Court's decision in this case. Subsequent jurisprudence has resulted in the extension of Batson to civil cases and cases where jurors are excluded on the basis of sex.)

The man John shot, who had been trying to intrude into their home, was an African-American. Since the victim would not be able to testify, his credibility would not be in issue; it would be very unlikely that Bill Wakely would be able to bring out the victim's criminal history and street gang affiliations. Therefore, they would not make a motion for a change of venue. The Lee County judge just might send the trial to Travis County – where it would undoubtedly end up with a divided, hung jury. The decision was made to keep the case in Lee County. John wanted to be found not guilty. He did not want a plea or a hung jury; the second trial could become an instant replay of the first.

On September 14th the arraignment was held. John pleaded not guilty. The judge said his docket was loaded with cases for the rest of the year. He said he did not like trying cases during holidays. He set John's trial for January 4th.

"Before your client leaves Mr. Wakely, I want to review this bond situation. The Probation Department tells me that you have been moving around, changing your appearance, changing ownership of property, and renting an old model car. Is your client planning to jump bail – or what?

John blurted out, "No Your Honor …."

Wakely grabbed John's arm, "Shush, please let me answer."

"No Your Honor, he is being threatened by the Austin Thug gang members."

"Well, I don't have time to adjudicate that. I'm going to make things a lot easier for the defendant. Sir, your bail is hereby revoked. You're remanded to the custody of the Lee County Sheriff for safe keeping until your trial. Good luck, Sir."

###

John could not for the life of himself remember being walked back into the jail cell he had only recently come from. It was nothing more than a metal cage with a bunk, toilet, and sink. The thought of having to live in such depravity until January made him feel ill. He sat on his steel bunk and gazed at the concrete floor.

He remained sitting in a shocked stupor for about an hour until an outer door opened and a deputy sheriff entered – escorting Elle. He immediately felt better.

"Thank God you came to see me. There was no way I could call you today. We only get three, ten-minute phone calls per week to family members. I can call Mr. Wakely; he can visit with me any time he wants."

"John, I had to see you. I cannot go back to our new home in Austin …."

"Elle, please remember they record all non-attorney, jail conversations."

"Thanks for reminding me Honey. I will be careful not to discuss your case. But, I cannot go home. I cannot stay there alone until January. I also know the Austin Thugs would come looking for you in Glenbrook and would find me all alone if I moved back there – helpless."

"I understand. Maybe you can live with Phyllis and Bruce for awhile."

"I know they would agree. But, it is not just that. We have been spending our retirement savings as if that money would last forever. There are the car rental payments, the new house rental payments, lawyer fees, and I cannot bring myself to mooch room and board from my sister and brother-in-law. Our Glenbrook home is turning into a white elephant. No one has even come to look at it. Real estate prices have tumbled ever since that damned virus raised its ugly head. The Austin gang banger nitwits are raising cane every single night. We still have to pay our real estate taxes, insurance, electricity, other utilities, and upkeep. I cannot handle what has happened to us. I do not want to live like this. This is not the life I had planned for."

"It is only going to be like this until January. We can tough it out for three months. Can't we? What is it you are trying to say?"

"I am trying to say that I still love you, but I love myself too. I cannot waste my golden years running from gangs, spending our retirement, and losing the life we worked so hard for. Remember, there is no guarantee you will be found not guilty. There is little doubt you shot and killed another person."

"My God Elle, I cannot believe this is happening. What do you want? A divorce? What?"

"I don't know, maybe I can stick it out until the trial. Maybe we need to talk again – during my next visit," she suggested as she began standing up.

The jail guard had been watching them through a glass window in his cell door. When he saw Elle stand up he entered and asked, "Y'all done visiting?"

Before John could say anything Elle replied, "Yes, we are done for now. Thank you for your help."

John looked stunned. Another, new wave of depression was sweeping over him. The message Elle had delivered was like a punch in the gut that he never saw coming. He realized she was hinting about getting a divorce. He could be facing this second tidal wave of his life – alone.

###

One of the jail guards John did not know by name could be seen coming down the hall. He was holding a key ring with at least a dozen oversize cell keys in his hands. When he was still some 15 feet away from John's cell door he announced, "Hey, you've got another visitor; you are a popular guy."

"He claims to be your lawyer, Bill Wakely. You're lucky to have him instead of one of the rookie assistant public defenders. Is that so? Should I bring him in?"

"Please. But, I know you folks record conversations with visitors. Could we have a private visit somewhere?"

"If Mr. Wakely asks me that he wants to visit with you in private, we can arrange it."

"Thanks. Please bring him back."

Wakely was probably in his mid-fifties. But, he looked physically fit and was a snappy dresser. He had on a dark blue suit, white shirt, jet black shoes, and a power tie. He would make a good impression on potential, primarily suburban, Lee County jurors.

Bill Wakely spoke first, "John, I feel sad about what happened to you. Being locked up like a wild animal must be pure Hell. But, at least you will be safe in here. Our sheriff is a straight shooter. Let me see if I can get us and attorney-client visiting room. Before they try to put us in your cell, let me go talk to the Sargent on duty."

Wakely stepped out of the cell block with one of the guards. He was gone for about ten minutes. When he returned he was with the Sargent John had seen earlier.

"John, Sargent Wilson was kind enough to let us use his own office. He won't be needing it for the next 15 minutes. Sargent, do you want us to follow you?

"Sure, I have some files and books in there, but there are three chairs and a desk you can use. Mind it I lock you two in here for security purposes?

Bill Wakely gave his consent and the two sat down while Wilson locked his office door. Wakely again spoke first.

"John, I met with your wife, Elle. You have a real keeper. She came to the office and told us you needed me. I quoted her my standard felony fee, she opened her purse, and handed me $10,000 in cash. So, we won't need to go over that sometimes awkward business. You were a practicing attorney before you retired. You would understand. Here is the deal. If there is a plea, I will refund $2,500 which is now in my trust fund. If we go to a bench trial, I get to keep that $2,500. If we go to jury, I would ask for another $5,000 – no matter how long the trial. If we were to lose, God forbid, you would be better served with a new attorney. You will be the boss on key decisions – whether we have a bench or jury, whether you plead not guilty or guilty. Is that all okay?"

"Yes. I totally understand. As you said, I used to do your job before I retired."

"Well, then, as you well know, we cannot have two pilots flying one plane. I will always discuss matters with you, but I will insist on trying the case. Okay?"

"Yep. Sounds okay."

"Here is the attorney-client contract we can read and both sign. There are two copies – one for each of us. The contract covers the fee arrangements and your copy will serve as your receipt for the cash. I already gave Elle a copy for her file. I think that will be enough business for today. I will come see you next week. At that time, we can discuss the case in detail. I already discussed many of the facts with Elle who was the only other person in your home during this incident. And, of course, I have newspaper clippings. At this time, it looks like you have reasons to be hopeful."

###

John felt more optimistic following the Wakely visit. "It sounds like you have reasons to be hopeful," kept ringing in his ears. Nevertheless, he knew neither a plea agreement nor a bench trial, without a jury, would be in the cards for him. No matter how pro-defense any plea agreement might be, he would nevertheless lose his law license. He was retired, but he and Elle had been hemorrhaging money ever since his arrest – without an end in sight. He might be forced to come out of retirement and resume the practice of law. One cannot practice law without a license. As far as having a bench trial, it would not be an option in his case. For starters, bench trials are often referred to by lawyers as a "slow plea of guilty." These racially tense times would put any judge in a "no win" situation. A guilty verdict would turn many voters in Lee County against him when he ran for reelection. A Not Guilty would send ACLU and every civil rights outfit in Texas down on him. The Thug Gang would seek revenge again. Not to mention, judges are not immune from being assassinated. He was looking forward to discussing jury trial strategy with Bill Wakely.

###

Less than a week had gone by since he had heard from Elle. After about four days had gone by, Elle came to visit. As she approached the glass window separating them, he noticed how really attractive she appeared for her age. And here he was, in an orange jump suit, feeling grubby because of the jail's two shower per week limit.

"Hello Elle, you cannot imagine how happy I am to see you. I have a thousand questions even without being able to discuss my case. As you know these visits are recorded – no privacy in this dump."

"I know. It is unbelievable that an innocent person has to spend over three months in jail. How are you doing?"

"I'm okay. But, now I can better understand what some of my former clients had to go through. More importantly, how are you doing?"

"Honey, do you remember our former neighbor, Sam Westergan? I met him again when I went to our former house that we decided to sell. I met the real estate sales lady there – to show her around. Sam has been very nice. He followed me over to Rent-a-Junk when I returned their car; and, he drove me over to our landlord's office to return his keys. I sure was glad we went with month-to-month rentals. Sam also took me over to Phyllis and Bruce's house where I am staying – where we were storing the Toyota."

"Sam Westergan? That guy has been trying to hit on you ever since we moved into Glenbrook. His wife left him and he would love to get something going with you."

"Oh, don't be silly. He is a nice man – trying to help me."

John, did not wish to show his jealousy. It is never becoming. But, what he had just heard was not good news. "Anything else new?"

"Yes, I also got a job at a real estate office. It is just secretarial. When Sally, the agent I've been dealing with in that office, and I met there, her boss told me Sally had filled him in on my dilemma and right then and there I got hired. The extra money comes in handy and it keeps me busy."

John did not want to ask too many questions, but this sounded disturbing. He dismissed his concern as jealousy. "You sure are doing very well. Do you miss me?"

"Of course, I'll come to see you as often as time permits. Well, I better be running. Love you," she quipped as she was picking up her purse and removing her car keys. The guard on duty opened the exit door when he saw her removing her keys, and he escorted her out of the jail.

###

It had been several days since Elle had come to visit when, at last, Bill Wakely came to visit. As usual, Bill had arranged for them to have a private attorney-client visit. As they entered the Sheriff's office, one could see the same layout – a desk with three chairs. For some unknown reason, when people once choose a chair, they always seem to return to it during a repeat visit – whether it happens to be a meeting room, dinner table, or easy chair in a living room. They sat in the usual places once again.

Wakely began by saying, "I hope you don't mind my dropping in to see you without a prior notice."

John decided to lighten the conversation, "Oh, I had a full schedule of appointments today."

Wakely smiled and began the discussion of the items he wished to discuss, "John, stop me if you disagree with anything I say about my plan for your defense. First, we agree any guilty plea is not in the cards for you. Second, with a political 'hot potato' case such as yours, the only logical choice for trial is going to be a trial by jury. Do we agree so far?"

"I agree. We touched on that before. What about the extra $5,000 fee – for a jury trial?"

"I plan to waive that part of the fee if you agree to the simplified jury trial plan I think would be in order given the facts. Let me explain the plan.

"That's great. What is your plan? I sure hope it doesn't lessen my chances for an acquittal."

"John, are you familiar with the U. S. Supreme Court's ruling in *Batson v. Kentucky*? We cannot stack a jury in our favor – especially in a case like this and at a time like this. You are obviously white and the guy you shot was a member of a black street gang that has been calling for the elimination of racial prejudice. Sadly, our county, though not as divided as Travis County, is nevertheless racially divided. If we were to allow the State to choose and all black jury, you would greatly increase the chance of being found guilty. If we had a 6-6 split in the jury's color, sadly we could end up with a hung jury and a second trial. My thinking we try to select as many white jurors as possible. If we exhaust our ten challenges, then we might be okay with an 11-1, 10-2, or 9-3 mix in our favor. It will be my job to ask questions that will disqualify as many jurors, who we do not want, as we can get away with. And, when we cannot get them excluded for cause, then we use peremptory challenges plus be prepared to give the court non-racial reasons. Do we agree?"

"Yes, in fact, this very same thought process crossed my mind. I find it very depressing that our legal system has come to this kind of thinking. You know, I represented many clients.

Yet, here I am, once again, using a legal, self-defense case, and using this technique. But, I guess we have to look at my act of shooting in Glenbrook and our legal self-defense tactics in the same light – self preservation. I am relieved we agree on jury selection strategy."

"In my opinion John, we have discussed our most difficult problem – jury selection. The facts of the case itself are really simple. A gang of lawbreakers tried to break into your home, you were there alone with your wife who was not an eyewitness to the shooting, but can set the stage – explain how the two of you felt – how fearful you both were. We can shorten and simplify the trial using stipulations that we know the State would not be opposed to. It is one of the reasons I feel comfortable waiving the $5,000 jury fee we had agreed on.

"There were lots of gang members, and only you to defend your home. Your military training taught you how to defend a building – shut off interior lights, arm yourself with the most effective defense weapon, and shoot before you or your loved ones get killed or seriously injured.

"You can explain how you learned in the military how to shoot to kill. Nevertheless, your intent that night was to simply stop that gang from violating your space.

"Elle will make an excellent witness. She is well spoken, cute, and smart. We cannot decide, not at this time, whether to use you as a witness. Maybe the DA will step in a hole an offer your exculpatory statement in evidence. If he does, you may not have to take the stand.

"We must remember, a jury will excuse mistakes – unless they come from a criminal defendant on the witness stand. If you agree, we are on the same page."

"Bill, we are on the very same page. I feel much better."

###

"Here Yea, Here Yea, the 156th District Court of Lee County, Texas, is now in session. The Honorable Robert Porter, District Judge, presiding. Please do not talk during these legal proceedings. And, please turn off your cell phones – unless you want me to confiscate them," announced the court bailiff in a bellowing voice.

John was seated at the counsel table furthest from the jury box as was customary. Bill Wakely was sitting beside him. The DA, and the arresting officer, were seated at the counsel table closest to the jury – as is customary.

The DA was the first lawyer to address the court, "Your Honor, we ask for a rule on witnesses." John knew that this motion was customary.

Judge Porter announced his ruling, "Ladies and Gentlemen, if there are any witnesses in the courtroom at this time, please do not enter this courtroom without the permission of this court. It is essential that witnesses not hear what other witnesses have to say. So, it follows, that should you see other witnesses anywhere during the trial, you are ordered not to discuss this case with anyone – including parties, other witnesses, and of course jurors. Doing so, in violation of this order could result in you being held in contempt of this court. Lawyers for the State and the defense are exempt from this ruling. They are allowed to talk to any witness in preparation. But, as these experienced lawyers well know, they are not allowed to tell their witness what other witnesses had to say. Thank you. Please raise you hand if you need a restroom break – at any time. We will accommodate your request."

John leaned over and whispered to Bill Wakely, "Where is Elle? I do not see her."

Bill tried to explain Elle's absence, "Both the DA and I have issued subpoenas for her. But, the Sheriff has not yet been able to find and serve her. However, on the phone, she promised she would appear. Is there any reason to believe she would not show up?"

"Well, no. But, I will admit I am a worry-wort and have seen stranger things happen during my years practicing law."

"John, there is no reason to have her standing around the courthouse during *voir dire*. If we need her, I will call her. And, I would assume the DA would also call her as a witness. After all, she was the only other person in your home at the time of this event."

"Okay Bill, please excuse my concern. It is not easy being a criminal defendant."

"I understand. It is a whole lot less stressful being one of the lawyers."

The judge again addressed those present, "Let us take a half-hour break. I have to powder my nose (everyone in the courtroom politely chuckles) and discuss a few things with the lawyers. But, please do not leave the courthouse."

###

(In chambers and outside the presence of the Jury)

"The Court is trying to move this case along. In my view, justice delayed is justice denied. I could not help overhearing Mr. Wakely and his client talking about a missing witness. Please tell me who is it? Bill, are you going to be asking for a continuance during the trial? If more time is needed, ask for it now – before we pick a jury."

"Your Honor, John noticed his wife was not here when you were admonishing the witnesses regarding the rule requiring them to stay out of the courtroom once the trial begins. We issued a subpoena for her to be here. She has not been served. But, John tells me there is no cause for concern. He feels certain she will be here with or without a subpoena when necessary. We will not be asking for any continuance. You can instruct her when she arrives."

"Does the Defendant agree with that?" asked the Judge (while looking at John for an answer)

"I understand," John answered. "She will be here."

"Okay, let the record show the defendant agrees with the decision of Mr. Wakely. Let's go back in there and start picking our jury."

(In the courtroom, with the Jury seated in an area usually reserved for spectators)

"Ladies and Gentlemen of the Jury, you will probably wonder why the Bailiff has given each of you a seat with a number on it. Each lawyer will given a chance to ask you some questions that you will answer under oath. I may also ask some questions. The lawyers may choose to challenge any one or more of you. You will then be asked to approach the Bench where the lawyers will state objections on which I will rule. We will embarrass no one. You may answer truthfully. Once it is determined there is no legal reason to excuse you, then each lawyer will decide whether or not to exercise one of his ten peremptory challenges. If you make it through that gauntlet, (everyone politely chuckles) you will then take a seat in the jury box. Today, we hope to pick 12 jurors and 2 alternate jurors. Are there any questions? Hearing none, we will begin the questioning."

###

After about six hours of questioning, all 14 jurors were selected. They were advised not to research any facts regarding the case, read newspapers, listen to the radio, or watch TV stories published by the media. They were also told the Court had business to attend to – with the lawyers – and they would stand in recess until the following morning.

(Back in the Court's Chambers with Judge Porter, the DA, Jeff Clinton, Bill Wakely, John, and the court's certified court reporter all present.)

"Counsel, before we swear in this jury, or start taking any testimony, the Court wants you two gentlemen to explain some potential *Batson v. Kentucky* jury picking issues. I am not happy, at least at this point, with the condition of our record. As it stands right now, our liberal appellate court might be just be able to find plain error – without either of you having made any specific objections. Let the record show, there are only three dark-skinned people in this group of 14 you have selected. Two are sitting among the 12 primary jurors, and one of the two alternates also appears to be an African-American. My concern is the DA has used all three of his ten peremptory strikes on black folks, and you know, both you lawyers should know, and the defendant, who has practiced in Lee County, should know darned well we cannot exclude jurors based on race. What do have to say about this? Please."

###

The DA, Jeff Clinton, spoke first, "Your Honor, we have worked together for a long time. You well know I do not have a biased bone in this body. We did not exclude white or black people from this jury based on racial reasons."

The Court: "We all know that Mr. Clinton. But, the appellate courts do not. They cannot take judicial notice, nor can I, that your peremptory challenges were valid. Why did you excuse black jurors? They all seemed to be well-qualified and they answered all your questions, and those of Mr. Wakely, very thoughtfully."

Clinton: "Let me look at my notes judge. (after a pause) Okay, here in my notes... I find that although #5 stated he would put his prior experience with police out of his deliberations and decisions, he did admit being stopped for what he called 'being black.' And, he did go on to say he understands why police patrol more aggressively in minority neighborhoods. But, my reason had nothing to do with his race. I did not want to ask him how the police treated him. That is why I struck #5.

"In regards to #18, my records show he has been arrested twice for DWI. One case was dismissed by my office. On the other, he was placed on probation, years ago, in Cook County, Illinois.

"In regard to #22, y'all may not have noticed it, but that woman was giving me dirty looks. I think she had come to my office and asked for a protective order against her live-in boyfriend several years ago. I did not want to dig into that matter here in a public courtroom. I felt she would not have appreciated that and would have held it against me."

Judge Porter: "Mr. Clinton, these people are all obviously African-American. Generally, prosecutors consider them to be pro-defense. So you can see why I wanted you to give legal, non-racial reasons for you striking them. We all know, *Batson v Kentucky*, does not allow racial-based challenges. But, I also find your reasons to be valid."

Porter: "Mr. Wakely, do you wish to make a record and object to my findings or ruling?'

Wakely: "No objection, Your Honor."

Porter: "Let the record show there are two African Americans seated in the Jury box – with the ten whites – and they will constitute our Jurors. Moving on to the alternates, one of the two is African American. We do have a properly selected panel."

John thought, "Judge Porter is a fox. He is trying to shield Wakely from my trying to allege ineffective assistance of defense counsel – in the event of my conviction."

Judge Porter: "All right, the court finds there were no *Batson* violations in the jury selection process. Let's get back to work."

###

(The parties re-enter the courtroom and take their places at counsel tables. Shortly thereafter, Judge Porter enters and takes his place on the bench.)

Judge Porter: "Counsel, are there any matters we need to discuss before I ask the bailiff to bring in the Jury?"

Jeff Clinton, DA: "There are Your Honor. Mr. Wakely and I have, with the approval of the Defendant, entered into written stipulations that should greatly simplify, and shorten, the length of this trial (handing the Court a copy). As you probably already know, many facts alleged in the indictment are not in controversy. But, before we ask you to read them to the Jury, we feel certain you would want to put the Defendant's approval on the record."

Judge Porter: "I appreciate very much the way you two experienced lawyers operate. Give me a moment to read this stipulation.

(There is an approximate five minute period of silence while the Court reads the written stipulation.)

"Okay, I have reviewed this document which I will ask the clerk to mark as 'Joint State and Defense Exhibit #1.' Mr. Ceres, I see you have signed these stipulations. Do you have any objections to them?"

"No objection."

"Do you fully understand that you have the right to have the State bring in witnesses to prove these matters?"

"Yes, I do."

"Did anyone pressure you to agree to waiving your right to confront witnesses on the facts being offered in evidence here – in written form – without cross-examination by your attorney, Mr. Wakely?

"No, Your Honor."

"And, finally, are you satisfied with the way your attorney, Mr. Wakely, counseled you on this stipulation matter?

"Yes, Your Honor."

"Then 'Joint State and Defense Exhibit #1' is admitted into evidence and will be read to the Jury when the Jury returns. Sargent Smith (Bailiff) please bring in the Jury."

The Court (after the Jury is brought in and seated)

"Ladies and Gentlemen of the Jury, the parties have entered into written stipulations regarding certain undisputed facts. This is often done to save time – not only for the parties – but to save your time, my time, their time and to focus everyone's attention on disputed questions of fact that you are here to resolve. These stipulations will be evidence and should be accepted by you as if they were testified to during your deliberations and as if you had heard them from the witness stand. Do you have any questions for the court? If so, kindly raise your hand."

(No hands are raised.)

THE COURT READS THE WRITTEN STIPULATION TO THE JURY

"The State of Texas, by its District Attorney, the Defendant, John Ceres, and his attorney, William Wakely, do stipulate and agree as follows: On June 24, 2020, at around 9:00 PM, the accused, John Ceres, and his wife, Elle Ceres, were sleeping in their bedroom when they were awakened by loud noises. They got out of bed and decided to find the source of the noise. John Ceres, armed himself with his legally-owned 45 cal handgun. He soon thereafter observed a group of young men as he was looking through the blinds of his patio window. John Ceres asked his wife to hide in either their study or bedroom – telling her he would handle the matter. It is further stipulated the Ceres home was located in Glenbrook, Lee County, in the State of Texas. The glass door of the patio was found broken and a man's leg was sticking through the opening caused by the broken glass when the police arrived. It was determined by the police and the Lee County Medical Examiner that the man had been shot in the leg by a 45 cal bullet that grazed an artery and which had caused him to bleed to death. The deceased was determined to be, Luther King Washington, age 20, date of birth January 3, 2000.

###

Judge Porter: "Counsel, do either of you wish to make an opening statement. The the indictment and the stipulation that have been read out loud and are now both circulating through our jury box... it probably gives the jury a pretty good idea of why we are here. But, counsel may want to supplement the stipulations with a short statement."

DA Clinton: "I have a few things Your Honor."

Bill Wakely: "Likewise, Your Honor, I have a short opening statement."

The Court: "Members of the Jury, please be advised that opening statements are not evidence. The attorneys may tell you what it is they intend to prove so that you can listen carefully to the witnesses for the facts they feel they can prove. Mr. Clinton, I do not allow rebuttal to opening statements. You may proceed."

OPENING STATEMENT BY DA CLINTON

"On June 24, 2020, at approximately 9:00 PM, Glenbrook Police Officers, Frank O'Hara and Demetrius Jones, responded to a 911 call that was dispatched to them by radio while they were on a routine patrol. The dispatcher notified them that a home break in was in progress and a gunshot had been heard.

"Upon their arrival at the Ceres home, we were greeted by Mr. John Ceres, the Defendant, who is seated next to his attorney at counsel table. Officer Jones will point him out to you when he testifies. The Defendant pointed to a leg that was sticking through the patio window. One could see blood on the pant leg.

Officer Jones asked if Mr. Ceres had called for an ambulance. The defendant stated he had not. When Officer Jones asked why he had not, the Defendant stated, 'Because he is dead.' Officer Jones asked the Defendant how he would know that, Ceres said he had first aid training while in the military and he had tried to find a pulse but could not find one. Ceres admitted he has had no other medical training.

The police arrested the Defendant for criminal homicide – for recklessly allowing the victim to die. At the close of this case, we will be asking you to find the Defendant guilty of Manslaughter – for which the accused has been indicted."

Judge Porter: "Mr. Wakely, are you going to make an opening statement?"

Wakely: "No sir. At this point, we have not decided whether to call any witnesses. It may become desirable when the State rests its case. As we all know from the *voir dire*, the defense has no burden to prove any facts. We will defer an opening statement at this time."

###

The trial proceeded without any surprises. The DA called the two Glenbrook police officers who repeated parts of the stipulation they had helped create. They emphasized their conversations with the Defendant wherein he admitted shooting the deceased with his 45 cal handgun, admitted he had "wasted" valuable time checking for a pulse – instead of calling an ambulance as soon as possible, and for concluding that the "victim" was dead – without any formal medical training. They added that the accused seemed very agitated and upset with how the police treated him.

Cross Examination of each officer by Defense Attorney Wakely: "Did you question Mrs. Ceres?

Both policemen answered identically, "Yes, but she told each of us she was hiding in the bedroom and did not see what had transpired."

Wakely: "In your police reports you both asked her why she was hiding, is that not so?

Both Police Officers: "Yes, we asked her. She stated she was "frightened" and told us her husband, the Defendant, had told her to hide in the bedroom and not turn on the lights. He would handle the matter."

Wakely: "Isn't it true that Mrs. Ceres told you she was 'terrified?'"

Both Police Officers: "Well, yes. Frightened or terrified... whatever?"

Wakely: "And your police reports both state the Defendant seemed very agitated? Because someone unknown stranger was breaking into their home?

DA: "Objection Your Honor – calls for repetitive and self-serving hearsay."

Court: "Denied."

DA: The State rests.

Court: "We are going to have a 15 minute recess. I am sure Mr. Wakely and his client need to discuss their strategy at this juncture."

###

JOHN AND ATTORNEY WAKELY PRIVATELY CONFER IN JUDGE PORTER'S CHAMBERS

John: "Bill, how do you think it is going?"

Bill Wakely: "John, I know you are on pins and needles; but, I feel we may have a victory on our hands. The facts already in evidence already contain our built in defenses of self-defense, lawful defense of another … Elle …, and defense of property. We do not want to risk pulling defeat from the jaws of victory. The State has proven a homicide; but, it has also proven your defenses."

John: "That may be legally sound, but do you think the jury may want to hear my side?"

Wakely: "Maybe, maybe not. But, if you testify, and some of them do not like your presentation, you could be found guilty. I seldom call my criminal clients to the stand. Attorneys who do, usually regret doing so – unless it happens to be necessary to establish a defense. That is not the case here."

John: "Bill, I am scared to death. But, I have chosen you as my attorney. I will agree to resting our case."

EVERYONE IS NOW BACK IN THE COURTROOM

Court: "Mr. Wakely?

Wakely: "The defense rests."

FINAL ARGUMENT OF THE DISTRICT ATTORNEY

After introducing himself to the Jury, the DA proceeded to point out the elements of the manslaughter offense alleged in the Indictment. Then, he pointed out to the Jury, how the stipulations, already in evidence, established the Defendant himself had admitted, on more than one occasion, that he had in fact shot Luther King Washington, the deceased, with his 45 cal handgun. He then read the findings of the Medical Examiner that established that the bullet from the Defendant's handgun had nicked a large artery in the victim's leg which caused him to bleed to death – while the victim was hanging, helplessly, in a patio window. He reminded the jury that the stipulation established the Defendant has no formal medical training but, nevertheless, decided to pronounce the victim dead before calling 911.

(THE DA, CLINTON, ADDED THE FOLLOWING TO HIS FOREGOING COMMENTS REGARDING THE STIPULATED FACTS)

"There was never any doubt that this shooting, and the death of Luther King Washington, the deceased, took place in Glenbrook, Lee County, Texas. There is no doubt the Defendant caused the death of our victim. There is no doubt the Defendant has no medical training. There is no doubt the Defendant took it upon himself to examine the victim and pronounce him dead – in spite of his lack of medical training. And, there was thereby created, by the Defendant, an unreasonable delay in calling 911. The State contends, in total, the Defendant acted unreasonably and recklessly as alleged in the Indictment. We ask you to return a verdict of guilty for the one and only count in the Indictment, specifically, GUILTY of MANSLAUGHTER."

THE COURT: "Mr. Wakely? You may argue."

WAKELY: *"Ladies and Gentlemen of the jury, in order to conform my argument in the style used by our District Attorney, I have only a few words to say. There is no doubt John was peacefully in his own home on the evening in question. There is no doubt John was bothering no one. There is no doubt John's wife was terrified by the aggressive, unlawful acts of Luther King Washington, the deceased, and his accomplices. There is no doubt that John was, at all times, acting in the defense of his wife, Elle, his home, and himself.*

"The Judge will instruct you that in the United States, and in the State of Texas, a person accused has no burden to prove his/her innocence. It is the State's burden to prove guilt in every criminal case beyond a reasonable doubt. In this case, there is no doubt that the State has failed in its burden. In fact, there is no doubt the evidence has established John's affirmative defenses of Self Defense, Defense of Another, and Defense of his property.

"We submit that justice calls for you to render the only just verdict... NOT GUILTY."

The Judge proceeded to instruct the Jury on the law pertaining to the case. The Bailiff directed the jurors to the jury's deliberation room, showed them where they could find the adjacent jury rest rooms, and advised them to knock on the courtroom door whenever they needed help or had reached a verdict.

After about seven hours of deliberations, during which people in the main courtroom could hear voices being raised, there was a knock on the door. The Bailiff returned to the courtroom and advised the Judge, "They are saying they cannot reach a verdict, Your Honor."

JUDGE PORTER: "Sargent Smith, bring the Jury into the courtroom."

(The Jury returned to the seats in the jury box they had occupied during the trial.)

JUDGE PORTER: "Do you have a foreperson?"

An African American woman who appeared to be about 50 years old stood up and identified herself as May Linda Brown who further advised the Court – without being asked – "We have a hung jury. We cannot agree on a verdict."

JUDGE PORTER: "This happens from time to time Ms. Brown. I will give you another instruction – orally and in writing – before I ask you all to return to the Jury Room for further deliberations. For those of you interested in the law, the law is well settled. The law has not changed over the years; *Allen v. United States*, 164 U. S. 492 (1896), was a United States Supreme Court case that, among other things, approved the use of a jury instruction intended to prevent a hung jury by encouraging jurors in the minority to reconsider.

JUDGE PORTER READS THE ALLEN INSTRUCTION

"Members of the Jury I'm going to ask that you continue your deliberations in an effort to reach agreement upon a verdict and dispose of this case; and I have a few additional comments I would like for you to consider as you do so.

"This is an important case. The trial has been expensive in time, effort, money and emotional strain to both the defense and the prosecution. If you should fail to agree upon a verdict, the case will be left open and may have to be tried again. Obviously, another trial

would only serve to increase the cost to both sides, and there is no reason to believe that the case can be tried again by either side any better or more exhaustively than it has been tried before you.

"Any future jury must be selected in the same manner and from the same source as you were chosen, and there is no reason to believe that the case could ever be submitted to twelve men and women more conscientious, more impartial, or more competent to decide it, or that more or clearer evidence could be produced.

"If a substantial majority of your number are in favor of a conviction, those of you who disagree should reconsider whether your doubt is a reasonable one since it appears to make no effective impression upon the minds of the others. On the other hand, if a majority or even a lesser number of you are in favor of an acquittal, the rest of you should ask yourselves again, and most thoughtfully, whether you should accept the weight and sufficiency of evidence which fails to convince your fellow jurors beyond a reasonable doubt.

"Remember at all times that no juror is expected to give up an honest belief he or she may have as to the weight or effect of the evidence; but, after full deliberation and consideration of the evidence in the case, it is your duty to agree upon a verdict if you can do so.

"You must also remember that if the evidence in the case fails to establish guilt beyond a reasonable doubt the Defendant should have your unanimous verdict of Not Guilty.

"You may be as leisurely in your deliberations as the occasion may require and should take all the time which you may feel is necessary.

"I will ask now that you retire once again and continue your deliberations with these additional comments in mind to be applied, of course, in conjunction with all of the other Instructions I have previously given to you."

The Jury retired once again to their jury room. As soon as they were out of sight and sound, John leaned over and asked his attorney, "Bill, I am scared shitless. Mrs. Brown, the foreperson, is one of the blacks on our Jury. I was never happy about us having to take her. Now, it looks like I am going to be found guilty or, at best, suffer a new trial following a hung jury. I cannot deal with being found guilty or having another trial. What do you think?"

"Stay cool. I can only try to imagine how you must feel; but, worry and fear will not help. Let's just take one step at a time. If it is a guilty verdict, you can appeal. If it is a hung jury, you can do it again – just like you have managed to endure this one. I still think we have a shot at not guilty. Good luck."

For about a half hour, no noise could be heard coming from its deliberation room. Then, one could hear voices being raised; but, the voices were not loud enough for the courtroom eavesdroppers to tell what the jurors were arguing about. A lull followed the arguments. Another half hour passed. Then, there was a knock at the door.

Judge Porter asked Sargent Smith to see what the jury wanted. The Bailiff asked the foreperson what she had to say.

May Linda Brown, the Jury Foreperson, answered, "We have a verdict."

Judge Porter: "Will, bring in the Jury."

THE JURY FILED BACK INTO THE COURTROOM AND TOOK THEIR USUAL SEATS

Judge Porter: "Ladies and Gentlemen of the Jury, I overheard you tell the Bailiff, Sargent Smith, that you now have a verdict. Ms. Brown, I see you probably remained the Foreperson – in that you are holding the verdict forms in your hands. Do you have a verdict?"

Ms. Brown: "Yes Your Honor, we have finally reached a unanimous verdict."

Judge Porter: "Sargent Smith, kindly bring the verdict forms Ms. Brown is holding to the bench."

The Bailiff handed the verdict forms to the bench. The Judge examined them closely. Then, he asked the Jury – one by one – "Is this your true and voluntary verdict?" As their names were called, each one answered in the affirmative, "Yes."

Judge Porter: "Having already polled each juror, the Court, finds their verdicts to be freely and voluntarily given. Now, therefore, in conformity with the verdict forms, the Court finds the Defendant NOT GUILTY. Mr. Ceres, you are released from your bond obligations. Of course, you will have to go through to Sheriff's standard procedures before you can leave the courthouse. Good luck sir."

###

"Hey Bill, there goes the foreperson, Ms. Brown. Could we ask her what caused the Jury's original report of a hung jury?"

"Sure John, frankly, I would also like to know what was going on."

"Say, Ms. Brown, would you mind answering a few questions for us?"

"No problem. The Judge told us we are now free to discuss your case, if we wish."

Bill spoke first, "Why do you think the Jury returned that hung jury report to the Court?"

"Well, we had a few white women on the Jury, as you know. A few of them do not approve of guns. And, a few, deplore violence – even in self defense. Those of us who live in 'the neighborhoods' had to educate them about what its like to live near these hoodlums; they keep us up all night, almost every night. You know there are times when my husband has had to sleep in a living room chair most of the night – with his 12 GA shotgun on his lap. He had to run those trouble-makers off a couple of times. We felt very sorry for Mr. and Mrs. Ceres. In my opinion, they were the real victims in this case. Eventually, after the Judge gave us that second round of instructions, the holdouts finally came around. Good luck to you and your Mrs. Mr. Ceres. And, congratulations on your good job defending him, Mr. Wakely."

"Thank you for visiting with us," John and Bill answered almost in unison.

(Mrs Brown, the foreperson, walked away – out of ear shot.)

"Boy did I have it wrong!" John horse-whispered to his attorney.

Wakely: "I guess a lot of people, including too many attorneys, have preconceived opinions about minority jurors. But, more and more of us are finding those who are most victimized by the recent violence and civil disobedience make the very best defense-oriented jurors – at least in this kind of litigation. That old 'black v white' theory no longer cuts the mustard."

###

The Bailiff escorted John back to the jail. Together, they gathered up the few personal items John was allowed to have in his cell. Then, John was escorted to the jail's administrative office where he would be able to sign out.

"Will I be allowed to call my wife for a ride?"

"Sure, you can use that phone on the desk."

John had removed his cell phone from its case hoping to call his wife's cell phone. But when he attempted to turn it on, it flashed a notice that the battery was not charged. The phone would not allow him to dial. So he went to the desk and used the phone on the desk that the Bailiff had earlier offered. However, upon dialing Elle's cell phone, her phone went directly to voice mail. He left no message. His only phone for incoming calls was his cell phone with a dead battery. At present, he had no home phone. He muttered some obscenities and hung up.

Using the desk phone, John called the number he kept on a note pad in his wallet for Elle's sister, Phyllis, and her husband, Bruce. He let it ring 8-9 times. No one answered. He tried again about five minutes later. This time Bruce answered. Bruce advised that Phyllis went shopping. He also advised that Elle no longer lived with them. He told John she had taken residence with a friend named Westergan. John thanked Bruce, asked how they were, and hung up.

"Say, Sargent Smith, I am having trouble reaching my wife. Could a deputy give me a lift to the Avis Car Rental office – right here in town?"

"Have a seat over there near the windows. I'll have to clear it with the duty Lieutenant in Command."

While he was seated waiting for a ride, John felt yet another wave of depression sweep over him. It was at least the second time he felt so helpless and disappointed – the first wave had hit him when he was locked in his cell – right after his initial arrest.

Sargent Smith, the Court Bailiff, received the okay from his superior. He took one of the squad cars from the motor-pool and dropped John off at Avis. John rented a mid-sized Chevy Cruz using his American Express Card. That card had a $25,000 credit limit. Elle was not a co-owner of that credit card. He had used it in his law practice – long before he even met Elle.

John realized, he finally had a lucky break. He would have enough resources for food, shelter, and transportation – at least for awhile. Eventually, he would find Elle and learn what he needed to know. Was their marriage kaput? Had she shacked up with Westergan? Would she be fair, as the executor of that trust they set up for house proceeds, would she agree to share the proceeds? But, he knew, Elle would not be able to answer the critical question – how could an innocent man end up in such a mess?

He drove the Avis rental car into Austin. There he found a room at a cheap, Hotel 8 at which he rented a room for three nights. He would take a nice hot shower, order a pizza, and get a good night's sleep. His Elle problems would have to wait until morning.

The morning air seemed cool – for Austin – when John stepped out of his motel room. The fresh air, and his new found freedom, raised his spirits. From his vantage point, he could see a Denny's restaurant about a quarter mile down the street. He would have a decent breakfast while his cell phone's battery was in his room charging. That cell phone had an extensive directory. After breakfast, he would try once again to call Elle and try to find out what was going on.

Elle answered on the first ring, "Hello, Sam?"

"No, sorry, it's me your husband."

"Oh, John, how are you doing?

"Well, I was found not guilty ... without any help from you."

"What do you mean? I did not receive any calls from Bill Wakely. John, could we meet somewhere, and have more time to talk?

"Sure, do you know where the Hotel 8 is located – on Park Lane close to a Denny's restaurant? It is almost 8:00 AM right now. Let's meet there and drive somewhere where we can sit down and talk."

"Okay. I'll see you there at 10:00 O'clock. I no longer have the Toyota. I'll be driving a dark gray Lexus. See you then."

(She hung up without saying anything more.)

At a few minutes before 10:00 O'clock, John locked his motel room and walked over to the Denny's parking lot. He saw a dark gray Lexus with Elle sitting at the wheel. He approached the tinted driver's window and confirmed it was Elle. He tapped on the window and Elle rolled it down.

"Hi John, why don't you go to the passenger's side and get in?"

John noticed she did not address him with any terms of endearment. She simply called him "John" as if they hadn't been husband and wife. He did not answer; he calmly walked around the rear end of the Lexus, opened the passenger door, and got in.

"Boy did you ever surprise me when you called my cell phone this morning. I didn't know you were being released."

"I guess, you thought I would be convicted. It didn't help that you blew off trying to call Bill Wakely. Wakely tried to call our old Glenbrook phone number; naturally it had been disconnected. I expected you to come in at the time the Judge directed or at least call Wakely. He gave you his business card didn't he?"

"John, please wait until we find a private place to talk. We have a lot to discuss. Where do you want to go?"

"Well, we are here at Denny's, the breakfast crowd is long gone, and the lunch people are probably not ready to have lunch. Let's ask for a fairly-isolated booth."

They asked the waitress of a corner table that had no one nearby. Elle began talking even before she had finished sitting down.

"John, you probably guessed by now; but, I've decided I cannot go on being married and living like we had been before you were incarcerated. We've lost our home, our car, and our reputation. You are going to be hounded by Austin gang members. I have been frighted ever since that June 24th shooting. We can continue to be friends – can't we?"

"But, I was trying to protect us. I have been found not guilty. We can move away from Austin and Texas. We can start over."

"There is something else. You have been locked up for a long time. I had to go back to work. I like my new job. I had to clean up the mess by selling our Glenbrook home and car. I like my new life."

"Aren't you going to mention Sam Westergan? Doesn't he play a part in your decision?

"I am glad you brought that up. Frankly, I have become very involved with Sam. I have become very fond of him."

"Okay, I get the message. What about the proceeds from the sale of the house and car? What do you plan to do about the proceeds?"

"There is nothing left from the sale of our Toyota. With the house proceeds, I had to pay the real estate agent, closing costs, title insurance, and moving expense. We had to pay Wakely $10,000 in legal fees. We lost money on the rent we had to pay Jackson and Rent a Junk. There is about $200,000 left. I think we should split what we have left 50-50."

"Okay, I guess that $100,000 plus that $25,000 line of credit, on my credit card, will keep me afloat. Maybe you could hire the attorney. Bolton and Wakely could handle our uncontested divorce for a reasonable fee. I trust them and I would not contest our agreement."

"John, I am so glad you are so reasonable. Maybe we can remain friends."

"Surely you are joking. Call me when you are ready to finalize our former relationship."

John got out of the Lexus and walked slowly back to his motel. While he was walking, he felt another wave of depression. He wondered how it was that his life, as he had known it, had ended. So much for one's right to self-defense.

###

As he sat in the motel room alone, John began to contemplate his options. He had just turned sixty years old. He had received a $1,500, less than reasonable, monthly pension from his former law firm. But, he knew that he could not live on that alone. In two more years, at age 62, he would be able to draw Social Security benefits of about $2,000 per month. And, in a few more years, when he would turn 65, he would be entitled to Medicare insurance. Meanwhile, he would have to supplement his firm's temporary medical insurance coverage, at least until age 65 when Medicare would begin to provide for health expenses. After the divorce, he would no longer be eligible basic coverage, as a dependent, on Elle's medical insurance.

Clearly, he would have inadequate income and insurance to enjoy the rest of his years – unless he re-activated his law license and returned to work. He knew that would be a waste of money at his age. Basically, he was now just another, aging, unemployed, perhaps uninsured, former lawyer – of which there are already far too many. He needed to consider other options.

Realistically, John had no savings to live off of. He would get that $100,000 dollars from Elle – for the remaining share of the proceeds from the sale of their Glenbrook home. And, he had a $25,000 line of credit available with his credit card. But, long term, he would have to do something drastic to live a decent life. The injustice he had suffered for defending his wife, their home, and himself, coupled with the loss of his wife, had destroyed the life he had once enjoyed – prior to pulling the trigger of his 45 ca handgun. He stretched out on the bed, turned on the TV, and fell asleep, as he remembered what Scarlet O'Hara said in *Gone With the Wind*, "I'll worry about that tomorrow."

###

The TV was still on when John woke up. At first, he felt he had had a bad dream. But, it was not a dream. His life had become a nightmare.

Then, while thinking about his options once again, he had a new, exciting idea. John's father had immigrated to the USA from Italy. His father obtained his citizenship from the USA by marrying John's mother who was a U. S. citizen. His father used to tell him about Italy. In the process, John learned he was entitled to apply for Italian citizenship – becoming a dual United States–Italian citizen.

About eight years ago, John, with the help of father's family, and the Internet, after nearly a year of hard work, John managed to obtain Italian citizenship. Pursuant to the European Union's founding agreement, that would entitle him to live and work in Italy, or any of the other 25 remaining EU countries (UK may not be included due to Brexit). Italy provides universal health care to all legal residents of Italy for a modest $500 per year premium. Outside the big cities, one can find a nice home for $30,000 or rent a decent apartment for $300-$400 per month. He now had a plan.

###

Using his cell phone, John found an affordable flight for under $500 – one way – via TAP AIR PORTUGAL, operated by United Airlines. TAP had the best all around option – via Lisbon – *AIR PORTUGAL, 2 stops, DFW to FCO for $489.*

Bill Wakely had called John and had asked him to pick up a cashier's check for $100,000 made payable to John. Elle also brought a box full of John's personal items – including his U. S. Passport and Italian citizenship papers. And, the best news of all, she had retained Bolton and Wakely to prepare the necessary divorce paperwork – which included the agreed property settlement that she and John had agreed to on that now fateful day following John's release from custody.

Perhaps because she was experiencing guilt about the way she had treated him, perhaps because of some residual affection for him, but for whatever reason, Elle had delivered on her promises. John made an appointment to stop by Bolton and Wakely to pick up his belongings and the settlement check.

Although he had been playing the "tough guy," John was suffering category one depression. He was happy about the fast progress in the divorce, the settlement check, and receipt of his personal items. But, Elle had been a big part of his life for a long time. And, he knew he still loved her. He was old enough to realize that more likely than not she was in a hurry to get rid of John in exchange for Sam Westergan. John knew he had little to offer her.

On returning to the Motel 8, he again stretched out on the bed and turned on the TV. This time, he opened a half-pint of Wild Turkey and had a few big swigs. After all. this was the end of one life and the beginning of another. He whispered to himself, "I'll worry about all this tomorrow."

After checking out of the motel, John drove to the Avis Rent a Car offices where he checked in the rental vehicle. One of the Avis employees, who was signing off for the day, witnessed the car return transaction and offered to give John a ride somewhere.

"Thank you so much. Please take me to the Austin airport. It is not far from here."

Once at the Austin airport, he knew he could book a Southwest Airlines flight to Dallas-Fort Worth (DWF) where he could connect with the two-stop (TAP) Portuguese airline (operated by United Airlines) - which would carry him to Rome's (FCO) International in Italy – Rome soon to be the site of his new home.

But once at the Austin airport, John first went to the United Airlines ticket counter to buy the tickets for Rome. After checking his U. S. Passport and his Italian citizenship papers, he was told the next flight to Rome would be the day after tomorrow.

John told the United agent, "That will work out well, and it will give me time to have Southwest Airlines to get me to DWF in a timely fashion."

"One last problem Mr. Ceres, I guess you heard about the corona virus pandemic?

"Who hasn't? It is all the news media has been covering."

"You are lucky you are a dual citizen. Italy has blocked all entries for non-Italian citizens. You will be able to enter Italy. But, all entries, even Italian citizens, are being required to quarantine for 14 days. Will that work for you?"

"I guess I do not have much choice. Here is the money for my tickets."

John handed the agent his credit card. The prices for the Southwest ticket were added to his credit card's debit charges for the Rome tickets. He received a printed receipts that are now used in lieu of tickets.

"You can get your boarding pass to Rome at the United Airlines Gate 3C. Have a nice trip sir. Thanks for flying United Airlines."

###

The flights to Rome were uneventful. The weather was clear and stable with only a few air bumps. John was pleased to learn from the crew that exceptional steps had been taken by the airlines to sanitize their planes after every flight. Although passengers were seated closely, they were seated in alternate seats and were asked to wear masks. The ventilation system had rapid circulation through HEPA filters.

Leonardo da Vinci Airport is one of the busiest international airports in Europe. When John's flight finally landed there, it was greeted by the usual airline service personnel plus a fairly large group of people who looked like civilian officials or undercover police. John learned a bit later that they were there to make sure that all passengers would be placed in quarantine for 14 days following their being cleared by customs and immigration officials.

"Passeggeri, se lasci questa quarantena senza permesso, potresti essere multato, incarcerato o espulso dall'Italia."

The foregoing warnings were repeated in English... *"Passengers, if you leave this quarantine without permission, you may be fined, jailed, or deported from Italy."*

(Italian officials passed out statistics and information regarding the dangerous corona virus.)

Global Cases

DEATH RATE 3.13%

Confirmed 30,181,110

Deaths 946,140

Italian Cases

DEATH RATE 12.17%

Confirmed 293,025

Deaths 35,658

The quarantine involved being housed in a vacant hotel which was no less comfortable no more spartan than the motel room he had rented in Austin. There was a restaurant nearby where the passengers could eat decent food – in shifts. Each passenger had to pay for his or her own food. "So far, so good."

###

The restaurant that was provided for passengers who were subject to quarantine had reached the capacity required for social distancing when John got there. Everyone who was not eating was wearing a mask. John got in line. The distance between diners waiting in line was more like three feet – rather than the required six feet. No one seemed to mind.

The passenger in front of him in line was a well-dressed, attractive woman. She appeared to be in her early fifties. John could not help noticing she had a trim figure. He hoped she would turn around so he could see her face. He decided to try speeding up the process.

"Isn't waiting in line, while in quarantine, fun?"

It worked, she turned around. She was wearing a mask. She had beautiful, gray-brown eyes common for Italian woman. She asked, "So you speak English?"

"Yes, I am an Italian-American – a dual citizen moving to Italy. My Italian is a bit weak and slow, but I speak both languages."

"Well, my English is weak and slow. So, I guess we can manage to communicate in the event they seat us at the same table."

John wasted no time, "Maybe we can ask to be seated at the same table. Maybe they would assume we were together. I'll ask, if you do not mind."

"No, I think that would be nice."

John was getting interested. He had earlier noticed she was not wearing an engagement or wedding ring. Maybe during dinner they would hit it off. Maybe her entire face was as lovely as her eyes. Maybe she had a sparkling smile.

"How long have you lived it Italy?"

"I was born and raised here – right here in Rome. It is still the biggest city in Italy. Tourists flock here in the summer. So, at times, it has even more residents than the official records. Where do you live?"

"Well, I am not a tourist. I have lived my entire life in the USA. But, my father was born in a small area on the Adriatic called San Benedetto del Tronto. I got my Italian citizenship recently through the Italian Counsel in the USA – citizenship by blood."

"You said you are not a tourist. Are you here on business?"

"No. About a month ago, my former wife divorced me. I always wanted to live in Italy. Maybe I read to many travel brochures. I am going to find a place and live here."

"My former husband, left me for a younger woman. We have a lot in common. I would be willing to show you around Rome. I think you would like living here. I know this city like the back of my hand. There are some beautiful places in Rome. And, the people are friendly."

"I would really like that. You are certainly one of those friendly Roman people. And, I must say very attractive. Would you be willing to give me your phone number. When we get out of this place I would really like to get to know you. You are right, we do have a lot in common."

"Sure. Here is one of my business cards. It has both my home and office phone numbers on it. How about visiting a little more here too – before we get out of quarantine? I am in Unit 2C."

"Great idea."

The couple continued getting to know each other during dinner. During dinner, they naturally removed their masks.

"The rest of your face is as pretty as your eyes."

"And, you are certainly as handsome as I had hoped while we were in line."

John walked her back to unit 2C and told her he planned to have lunch at the same place tomorrow. He asked her to meet him at about 11:30 AM – Roman time. They agreed to what might become their "first date." Perhaps this new acquaintance would not develop into a new relationship. But, on the other hand, perhaps it would.   A new wave swept over him as he was about to fall asleep that night. But, this time, it was a new, powerful wave of happiness. This just might be *The Last Wave.*

ABOUT THE AUTHOR JOE COLLINA

Joe Collina's legal name is Joseph V. Collina. He was born in April 1938, in Chicago Heights, Illinois. His undergraduate BS degree was received in 1961 from Purdue University. He served six years in the Army Reserves during which time he worked for the Andrew Corporation in Orland Park, Illinois, in the production of helix cables and antennas, while attending graduate business school at Northwestern University's during evening classes. In 1967, the author received an MBA degree in marketing from Northwestern University.

Upon graduation from Northwestern, Collina was one of four sales representatives covering three states selling electric motors for OEM and replacement applications. While employed in the marketing of electric motors, the author attended evening classes at John Marshall Law School where he met his wife of forty-five years. The author, and his wife Mary, graduated with JD degrees and practiced law for the following 32 years.

Now retired, the author writes as a hobby. He has a daughter and four grandchildren who also made their homes in Tennessee. While practicing law, the author tried countless civil and criminal cases. He served as a chief public defender and a supervisor in the offices of the Lake County State's Attorney.

The author is a dual citizen of the USA and Italy.